KT-423-373

The Key

ROSAMUNDE PILCHER

A Phoenix Paperback

The White Birds and
The Tree first published
by Hodder and Stoughton in 1990.

This edition published in 1996 by Phoenix
a division of Orion Books Ltd
Orion House, 5 Upper St Martin's Lane, London WC2H 9EA

Copyright © Rosamund Pilcher 1984, 1985

Rosamunde Pilcher has asserted her right to be identified as
the Author of this Work

All rights reserved. No part of this publication may be
reproduced, stored in a retrieval system, or transmitted,
in any form or by any means, electronic,
mechanical, photocopying, recording or otherwise,
without the prior permission of the copyright holder.

ISBN 1 85799 748 4

Typeset by Deltatype Ltd, Ellesmere Port, Cheshire
Printed in Great Britain by
Clays Ltd, St Ives plc

Contents

THE KEY

The Key

A long time ago, the village had slept, remote and rural, at the foot of the Cotswolds, but as main roads stretched out from London, and more and more city people sought the serenity of the country, it had gradually changed.

The family grocer was taken over by a national supermarket, and the butcher's premises were bought out by an antique dealer. As well, there were now a little dress shop, inordinately expensive, and a couple of estate agents.

On a Saturday morning in June, a car turned the corner at the foot of the long street, and made its way slowly up the gentle incline, shaded by lofty trees. At the wheel was a girl, slender, dark-haired, quite young; she had driven that morning from London. Now, as she drove, she leaned forward to scan the names above the shop fronts, and when she saw the estate agents' office, she drew into the road side, parked carefully, and turned off the engine.

She got out of the car, crossed the pavement and let herself in through the glassed door, to find herself in a modern office where a young man sat behind a desk.

He smiled, ready and willing to help this tall, pretty young woman, and got to his feet.

'Good morning.'

'Good morning. I'm sorry to bother you, but I'm looking for a house. It's called Stenton, and it's in this village . . .'

The young man did not wait for more. 'Of course,' he said at once. 'You want to go and see the house.'

'Yes, but . . .'

The young man, trained in salesmanship, over-rode this mild hesitation. 'Do we have your name?'

'It's Ruth Conway, but I haven't phoned or anything, so you won't have any record.'

'I see.' He smiled again. 'What I call an impulse viewing. You won't be disappointed, I'm sure. It's a charming little house and fully furnished.'

'It's . . .' She hesitated again, searching for the right words. 'You said it was a *little* house?'

'Used to be part of a stable complex.'

'But there's a big house, too?'

'That's a ruin now. It burned down about three years ago. Just after the old lady, who had lived there all her life, died.'

'But – how? Why?'

'An electrical fault, and because the house was empty at the time there was no one to raise the alarm. The first the village knew of the tragedy was seeing the flames leaping from the roof. And, of course, by then it was too late. It was a very old house; Elizabethan, you know, and panelled throughout. It went up like tinder.'

There was a pause while Ruth Conway digested this information. Then she said, 'I didn't know.'

'How could you?'

Now he looked at her more closely. She was wearing a pleated skirt and a navy blue sweater. Her legs were beautiful, very long and slender, and around her neck – and this was almost more eye-catching than the legs – was a gold chain. From this hung a heavy round medallion, depicting the embossed head of a man. It looked, to the assessing eye of the young agent, both old and genuine. He wondered how she had come by such a thing.

She said, 'The other house – the little one that's for sale –'

'For rent,' he corrected her quickly.

'Would I be able to see it?'

'Yes, I think so. The only thing is –' he pushed back a starched cuff, consulted a silver watch – 'I have a client coming in at any moment, so I wouldn't be able to come with you.'

'Could I go by myself?'

He looked surprised and a little put out. 'I – I should think so. I'll find out. If you'll just wait for a moment, I'll make a phone call.'

He took himself off into some back office to make the necessary phone call, although there was a perfectly good telephone right there on the desk. Ruth waited. Presently he reappeared, all smiles.

'That'll be all right. Here we are.' He opened a drawer and produced a key with a chain and a little label. She took it from him, and stood with it in the palm of her hand, her head bent, her face hidden from him by that fall of heavy dark hair. 'Now,' he said, 'do you know how to find the house?'

She raised her head. 'I've no idea.'

'Never been here before?'

'No.'

'Excuse my asking, but you're an Australian, aren't you?'

'Yes, I am. My father has a sheep station about fifty miles from Melbourne.'

'Is this your first visit to Britain?'

'Yes.'

'Enjoying it?'

'Yes. Very much.'

The young man went to open the door and together they stepped out into the sunny, flower-scented afternoon.

'Up the street,' he told her. 'Past that last big house and then take the small lane to the right. That leads to the gates of Stenton. You go up the drive as far as the house, and you'll see the stables on your left.'

'You've been very helpful. I'll bring the key back.'

'Yes, please. And if I'm not here and the office is locked, then just drop it through the letter-box. And if you're interested in the house, perhaps you could give me a telephone call later on in the afternoon. I don't shut up shop until five. Here . . .' He felt in some inner pocket. 'My card.'

She took the card, and read his name and telephone number. He was called, she saw, W. T. Redward. Back behind the wheel of her car, heading up the street in the direction he had indicated, she had time to feel a little guilty about W. T. Redward as one must about any person one has deceived, however harmlessly.

But there were other and more absorbing things to occupy her mind, and the guilt lasted only for an instant. She reached the turning and found herself in a narrow lane which curved away between grassy banks and an avenue of beeches. As she came around the curve, an immense pair of gateposts reared up before her, and she knew then that she had come to Stenton.

The driveway was short, and almost at once the sad ruin came into view, set back beyond a stretch of rough grass which must once have been a lawn of velvet smoothness. The drive divided and circled this, to meet again in a gravelled carriage sweep, but here again weeds grew rampant, and brambles twined with the ancient unpruned roses which still clung to the broken walls of the house.

She stopped the car and got out. The place had an air of desolation, of quiet, as though caught in a vacuum of silence and decay.

She looked at the roofless, eyeless wreck of the old house and felt sad. Here families had lived, children had played, aproned maids had carried tea-trays; babies had been born, old men had died. Here had laughed young girls in white muslin, dressed for their first parties, with the house filled with music.

She began to walk across the gravel, her footsteps alarmingly loud on the loose stones. It had rambled, this old house. One wing had been razed to the ground, but the centre section still stood as tall as the first floor, with the ornate doorway set beneath a giant slab of golden Cotswold stone. The door was oak, and ajar. Cautiously, Ruth went forward and pushed it gently inwards.

It moved with a creak. Beyond lay what had once been the hallway, but the floor was broken and charred, exposing great voids of black space, so there could be no question of going farther. But the great stone fireplace still stood, and the remains of an enormous staircase.

She was filled with frustration. Having come so far, she could go no farther. The place was a death trap. After a little she backed away, pulling the door shut behind her. She turned, and saw the man walking across the grass towards her.

His hair was dark and curly and a black Labrador ran at his heels. As Rush stepped out from under the doorway the Labrador barked, but the man quietened him with a movement of his hand.

'It's dangerous,' he told her. 'You mustn't go in. I put up a Keep Out sign, but the boys from the village must have knocked it down.' He had a thin brown face, dark eyes and an unmistakable air of distinction.

'Have you come to see the stable house? You're Miss – Conway, I think Mr Redward said.'

'Yes. Ruth Conway. Was it you he telephoned?'

'Yes. I'm Gavin Armitage.'

'Do you own all this?'

'Yes.' He smiled then, wryly, but it changed his whole rather forbidding appearance. 'What remains of it.'

'I can't bear it.' She turned back to look at the sad, scarred face of the old house. 'It must have been so beautiful.'

'It was.'

'Mr Redward told me it burnt down after the last owner died.'

'Yes.' He added, as though it were of no consequence, 'She was my grandmother. She loved the house almost more than life itself. She'd been born here and she was married from the house, and she had all her children here, and she lived here as a widow, and she finally died, quite peacefully, in her own bedroom.'

'Was she an only child?' Ruth prompted.

'No. She had a brother and a sister. The brother was killed in the First World War, and the sister eloped with the gardener's boy and was never heard of again. So when my grandmother married, her father made Stenton over to them. But it was always her house. From beginning to end, it was her house.'

'She must have been a lady of some means to have kept a place this size going.'

'She didn't have means so much as determination. After she was widowed, she decided that nothing would make her give up the house, so she opened it to the public. Summer Saturdays and Sundays you could scarcely move for visitors, and my grandmother was always there, either showing people around, or brewing up another urn of tea, or talking flowers to any person who showed the slightest interest.'

'She sounds fun.'

'She was.'

'And now it all belongs to you?'

'Yes. My father's still alive, but he lives and works in London. For some reason Stenton never meant that much to him. But my grandmother knew that I loved it just as much as she did. She wanted me to live here. But the old house had other ideas. It was uncanny. As though it didn't want anyone but her to live here . . .' His voice died away. And then, with a smile that was both apologetic and faintly embarrassed: 'Don't know why I'm talking so much. You've come to see the stable house, not to have your time wasted.'

'It's not wasting time, I assure you. Go on telling me. Where do you live?'

'That was no problem. Stenton isn't just a house, it's an estate, with a farm. I live in the farmhouse and try to make the land pay its way. It's a struggle. But that's why I want to let the stable house.'

She said nothing to this. After a little, in a changed tone of voice he said, 'You know, you sound like an Australian.'

'That's because I am one.'

'Why should you want to rent a house in the Cotswolds?'

She shrugged. 'I just do.'

'Come along then. I'll take you to see it.'

She followed him and the dog around the side of the charred walls to where, within an old stable-yard wall, a cottage had been newly converted. The windows were bright, the roof re-tiled, the front door painted a cheerful blue.

'Have you got the key?'

Ruth took it from her pocket and gave it to him. He opened the door, and she followed him inside.

'That's the sitting-room, and then beyond it the kitchen-dining room. This faces east, so you'll get all the morning sun. And there's a utility room in here . . .' He opened a door, and they peered inside. Clothes washer and a dryer. And upstairs –' she followed his long legs up a steep stairway, carpeted in cherry red – 'there are three bedrooms, two with basins, and a bathroom, and an airing cupboard.'

Downstairs again, they returned to the sitting-room. 'There's central heating, of course, but an open fire as well. If you like, I can sell you logs from my saw-mill . . .'

The words tailed off. A silence fell between them. Standing

there, all at once neither of them had anything left to say to the other. Ruth, staring determinedly at the empty fireplace, felt his eyes upon her. After a bit, she looked up and met them.

'What a farce this is!' he remarked. 'You're not interested in renting this place, are you?'

She shook her head. 'I got talked into coming by W. T. Redward.'

'That's no answer. There's something fishy going on.'

'What makes you say that?'

'Finding you nosing around the ruins of the house. And this – I noticed it at once.' And he reached out a hand and took up the heavy old medallion, holding it in his palm.

She looked back into his face. His dark eyes were watchful.

'What does that tell you?'

'My grandmother had the twin of it. I have it now. Mine is the head of a woman. I think they must have been struck as a love token, or a seal of engagement. They're very old and very valuable. My great-grandfather brought them back from Italy, and gave one to each of his daughters, as an eighteenth birthday present. So this one belonged to . . .'

'Amy,' said Ruth. 'The one who eloped with the gardener's boy and was never heard of again. *My* grandmother.'

'What became of her?'

'They sailed to Australia, and they married. The gardener's boy was my grandfather.'

'Did they make a success of their life together?'

'Very much so. Although he was a man of humble birth and, I suppose, little formal education, he was a hard worker and he had a sort of natural astuteness. In time he bought land, raised sheep, built a house. That grew into the sheep station where I was brought up. My father still runs the place. It's called Turramoolagong.'

'Turramoolagong,' he repeated, and began to laugh.

'What's so funny?'

'I never realised I had a second cousin called Ruth Conway living in a place called Turramoolagong. Life is full of surprises.'

'Second cousins? I suppose we are.'

'How long have you been in this country?'

'Just six months. My grandmother died and left me a little money. She said in her Will it was to pay my fare back home, as she resolutely called England all her life. And I'd trained as a nurse, working mostly with children, so living in London I can earn my keep, and more, being a nanny. I've got a good job right now, for three months – this is just my weekend off – but when this job is finished I hope I'll have saved enough to get around and see a bit of the country.'

'But why Stenton? Why did you come to Stenton?'

'Oh, Gavin . . .' His name came out quite naturally, as though she had been using it for years. 'If only you knew how much I know about the place. Granny used to talk on and on about how it used to be when she was a girl, and I would listen forever, hearing about the parties and the picnics and the Christmases, with a tree in the hall so tall that it reached to the third landing. I knew how the house looked, every brick and stone of it, long before I drove the car through the gates. That was why I wanted to go in, and be there. Walking through the rooms, even if they were ruined and charred and windowless. But of course I couldn't even do that.'

'I'm sorry.'

For what?'

'That the house, like the two old ladies, is dead.'

All this time, as they talked, he had been holding the medallion. Now he let it go, and she felt its weight drop against her breast. 11

'So what happens now?' he asked.

Ruth shrugged. 'I return the key and drive back to London.'

'But you've got a weekend off. Don't you want to stay? Stay,' he pressed her. 'Not in a pub or an hotel, but with me. I've masses of space and a guest room – also a housekeeper.'

'What will your wife say when I turn up?'

'Blessed girl, I haven't got a wife.'

'I'd like to stay,' she said simply. 'I think we've got a lot to talk about.'

'Yes, I think we have. And I want to show you the twin to your medallion,' he said. 'And we can pore over old photograph albums and read old diaries and wallow in nostalgia.'

He then leant forward and set a kiss upon her mouth, a swift and unpassionate kiss that was more a greeting than a gesture of affection.

In Ruth's car, with Gavin behind the wheel, and the black Labrador sitting up in the back seat like a person of much importance, they drove back to the village and the estate agents' office. Ruth got out of the car and crossed the pavement to try the door. It was, however, locked. W. T. Redward had not yet returned. She took the key out of her pocket and . . .

For a moment she hesitated, thoughtful, standing there with the key in the palm of her hand. A very ordinary little latchkey, opening the door to an ordinary house which she had never even wanted to see. But it had opened other doors as well, perhaps changing the whole course of her life. A door to the past. A door to the future. Who could tell?

She smiled, and dropped the key through the letter-box, and then turned and went back to where he waited for her. Her second cousin. Her new friend. Gavin.

THE WHITE BIRDS

The White Birds

From the garden, where she was engaged in cutting the last of the roses before the frost set in, Eve Douglas heard the telphone ringing inside the house. She did not instantly rush indoors, because it was a Monday, and Mrs Abney was there, pushing the vacuum cleaner around like a mad thing and filling the house with the smell of furniture polish. Mrs Abney loved to answer the telephone, and, sure enough, a moment later the sitting-room window was flung open to reveal Mrs Abney, waving a yellow duster to attract Eve's attention.

'Mrs Douglas! Telephone.'

'Coming.'

Carrying the prickly bunch in one hand and her secateurs in the other, Eve made her way up the leaf-strewn grass, shucked off her muddy boots, and went indoors.

'I think it's your son-in-law, from Scotland.'

Eve's heart gave a faint lurch. She put the flowers and the secateurs down on the hall chest and went into the sitting room. The furniture was all over the place, the curtains draped over chairs to facilitate floor-polishing. The telephone stood on her desk. She picked up the receiver.

'David?'

'Eve.'

'Yes?'

'Eve . . . look . . . it's Jane.'

'What's happened?'

'Nothing's happened. It's just that we thought last night that the baby was coming . . . and then the pains sort of stopped. But this morning the doctor came, and her blood pressure was a bit high, so he's taken her into hospital . . .'

He stopped. After a little Eve said, 'But the baby isn't due for another month.'

'I know. That's it.'

'Do you want me to come?'

'Could you?'

'Yes.' Her mind flew ahead, checking the contents of the deep freeze, cancelling small appointments, trying to work out how she could abandon Walter. 'Yes, of course. I'll catch the five-thirty train. I should be with you at about a quarter to eight.'

'I'll meet you at the station. You're an angel.'

'Is Jamie all right?'

'He's all right. Nessie Cooper's keeping an eye on him; she'll look after him till you get here.'

'I'll see you, then.'

'I'm sorry to have to spring this on you.'

'That's all right. Give Jane my love. And, David . . .' She knew it was a ludicrous thing to say, even as she said it. '. . . try not to worry.'

Slowly, carefully, she replaced the receiver. She looked up at Mrs Abney, who stood in the open doorway. Mrs Abney's cheerful expression had gone, to be replaced by one of anxious concern which Eve knew was mirrored by her own. There was no need for spoken word of explanation. They were old friends. Mrs Abney had worked for Eve for more than twenty years. Mrs Abney had watched Jane grow up, had come to Jane's wedding wearing a turquoise two-piece and a matching turban hat. When Jamie was born, Mrs Abney had knitted him a blue blanket for his pram. She was, in every sort of way, one of the family.

She said, 'Nothing's gone wrong?'

'It's just that they think the baby's on the way. It's a month early.'

'You'll have to go.'

'Yes,' said Eve faintly.

She had been going to go anyway, had everything planned for next month. Walter's sister was going to come up from the south to keep him company and do the cooking, but there could be no question of her coming now, at such short notice.

Mrs Abney said, 'Don't you worry about Mr Douglas. I'll keep an eye on him.'

'But, Mrs Abney, you've got enough to do – your own family . . .'

'If I can't make it in the mornings, I'll nip up in the afternoons.'

'He can make his own *breakfast* . . .' But somehow that only worsened the situation, as though poor Walter was capable of nothing more than boiling an egg. But it wasn't that, and Mrs Abney knew it. Walter had the farm to run; he was out working from six o'clock in the morning until sunset or later. He needed, got, and consumed meals of enormous proportions because he was a big man and a hard-working one. He took, in fact, a good deal of looking after.

'I – I don't know how long I'll be away.'

'All that matters,' said Mrs Abney, 'is that Jane's all right and the baby too. That's your place . . . that's where you've got to be.'

'Oh, Mrs Abney, what would I do without you?'

'Lots of things, I expect,' said Mrs Abney, who was a true Northumbrian and didn't believe in showing emotion. 'And now, why don't I make a nice hot cup of tea?'

The tea was a good idea. While she drank it, Eve made lists.

17

When she had finished drinking it, she got out the car, drove the short distance to the local town, went into the supermarket and there stocked up on all the sort of food that Walter could, if necessary, cope with for himself. Tins of soup, quiches, frozen pies, frozen vegetables. She stocked up on bread, butter, pounds of cheese. Eggs and milk came from the farm, but the butcher wrapped chops and steaks and sausages, found scraps and bones for the dogs, agreed to send a van out to the farm should the need arise.

'Going away?' he asked, slicing a marrow bone in two with his cleaver.

'Yes. Just up to Scotland to stay with my daughter.' The shop was full and she did not say why she was going.

'That'll be a nice change.'

'Yes,' said Eve faintly. 'Yes, it will be very nice.'

She got home and found Walter, who had come in early, sitting at the kitchen table and eating his way through the stew, boiled potatoes, and cauliflower cheese which Mrs Abney had left for him in the bottom oven of the Aga stove. He wore his old working clothes and looked like a ploughman. Once, and it seemed a long time ago, he had been in the Army; Eve had married him as a tall and dashing captain, and they had had a traditional wedding with herself in flowing white and an archway of swords awaiting them as they emerged from the church doorway. There had followed postings in Germany and Hong Kong and Warminster, always living in married quarters, never having a home of their own. And then Jane arrived, and soon after that Walter's father, who had spent his life farming in Northumberland, announced that he had no intention of dying in harness, and what was Walter going to do about it?

Eve and Walter made the great decision together. Walter

said goodbye to the Army, spent two years at an Agricultural College, and then took over the farm. It was a decision neither of them regretted, but the hard physical work had left its mark on Walter. He was now fifty-five, his thick hair quite grey, his brown face seamed with lines, his hands permanently engrained with engine oil.

He looked up as she appeared, borne down with laden baskets. 'Hello, darling.'

She sat down at the other end of the table without even taking off her coat. 'Did you see Mrs Abney?'

'No, she'd gone before I came in.'

'I have to go to Scotland.'

Across the table their eyes met. 'Jane?' said Walter.

'Yes.'

The sudden shock of anxiety seemed, visibly, to drain him, to diminish him in some horrible way. Every instinct was to comfort him. She said quickly, 'You mustn't worry. It's just that the baby's going to arrive a little early.'

'Is she all right?'

Matter-of-factly, Eve explained what David had told her. 'These things happen. And she's in hospital. I'm sure she's getting the best of attention.'

Walter said what Eve had been trying not to tell herself ever since David's telephone call. 'She was so ill when Jamie was born.'

'Oh, Walter, *don't* . . .'

'In the old days she'd have been told never to have another child.'

'It's different now. Things are so different. The doctors are so clever – ' she went on, vaguely, trying to reassure not only her husband, but herself. 'You know . . . scans and things . . .' He looked unconvinced. 'Besides, she wanted another child.'

'We wanted another child, too, but we only had Jane.'

'Yes, I know.' She got up and went to kiss him, putting her arms around his neck, burying her face in his hair. She said, 'You smell of silage.' And then, 'Mrs Abney will take care of you.'

He said, 'I should be coming with you.'

'Darling, you can't. David knows that, he's a farmer himself. Jane knows it. Don't think about it.'

'I hate you having to go alone.'

'I shan't be alone. I'm never alone as long as I know that you're around somewhere, even if it's a hundred miles away.' She drew away from him, and smiled down at his upturned face.

'Would she be so special,' Walter asked, 'if she hadn't been an only child?'

'Just as special. No person could ever be as special as Jane.'

When Walter had taken himself off, Eve busied herself, putting the shopping away, making a list for Mrs Abney, stacking up the deep freeze, washing the dishes. She went upstairs to pack a suitcase, but when all this was accomplished, it was still only half-past two. She went downstairs and pulled on her coat and her boots and whistled up the dogs, then set off across the fields towards the cold North Sea and the little sickle of beach which they had always thought of as their own.

It was October now, still and cool. The first frosts had turned the trees to amber and gold, the sky was overcast, and the sea grey as steel. The tide was out, the sand lay smooth and clean as a newly laundered sheet. The dogs bounded ahead, leaving trails of paw-marks in the pristine sand. Eve followed, the wind blowing her hair across her face, humming in her ears.

She thought of Jane. Not now, lying in some anonymous hospital bed waiting for God knew what was going to happen. But Jane as a little girl, Jane growing up, Jane grown up. Jane with her tangle of brown hair and her blue eyes and her laughter. The small, industrious Jane, sewing dolls' clothes on her mother's old machine, mucking out her little pony, making rock buns in the kitchen on wet winter afternoons. She remembered Jane as a leggy teenager, the house filled with her friends, the telephone endlessly ringing. Jane had done all the maddening, harum-scarum things that all teenagers do, and yet had never herself become maddening. She had never been plain, never sulky, and her natural friendliness and vitality ensured that there had never been a time when she had not had some adoring male in attendance.

'You'll be getting married next,' Mrs Abney used to tease her, but Jane had ideas of her own.

'I'm not getting married until I'm at least thirty. I'm not getting married until I'm too old to do anything else.'

But when she was twenty-one, she had gone to spend a weekend in Scotland, and had met David Murchison and fallen instantly in love, and the next thing Eve was in the thick of wedding plans, trying to work out how the marquee was going to fit onto the front lawn and searching the shops of Newcastle for a suitable wedding dress.

'Marrying a farmer!' Mrs Abney marvelled. 'You'd have thought, being brought up on a farm, you'd have had enough of that sort of life.'

'Not me,' said Jane. 'I'm jumping out of one dung-heap into another!'

She had never been ill in her life, but she was very ill when Jamie was born four years ago, and the baby had been kept in intensive care for two months before he was allowed home. Eve had gone to Scotland at that time, to take care of the little household, and Jane had taken so long to recover and get back her strength that privately Eve prayed that she would never have another child. But Jane thought differently.

'I don't want Jamie to be an only child. It isn't that I didn't adore being one, but it must be more fun to be one of a family. Besides, David wants another.'

'But, darling . . .'

'Oh, it'll be all right. Don't fuss, Mumma. I'm as strong as a horse, it's just that my insides don't seem to be very cooperative. It only goes on for a few months, anyway, and then you've got something marvellous for the rest of your life.'

The rest of your life. The rest of Jane's life. All at once Eve was gripped in a freezing panic. Two lines of a poem she had once read rose from her subconscious and rang through her head like a roll of drumbeats:

> *Unstoppable blossom*
> *above my rotting daughter . . .*

She shivered, chilled to the bone, overwhelmed by every sort of cold. She was now out in the middle of the beach, where an outcrop of rock, invisible at flood tide, was revealed, abandoned like a wrecked hulk by the sea. It was crusted with limpets, fringed with green weed, and on it sat a pair of herring gulls, beady-eyed, screaming defiance at the wind.

She stood and watched them. White birds. For some reason white birds had always been an important, even symbolic, part of her life. She had loved the gulls of childhood, sailing against the blue skies of seaside summer holidays, and their cry never failed to evoke those endless, aimless sunlit days.

And then there were the wild geese which, in winter, flew over David and Jane's farm in Scotland. Morning and evening the great formations crossed the skies, skimming down to settle on the reedy mudflats by the shores of the great tidal estuary that bordered David's land.

And fantail pigeons. She and Walter had spent their

honeymoon in a small hotel in Provence. Their bedroom window had faced out over a cobble courtyard with a dovecote in the centre of it, and the fantails had woken them each morning with their cooing and fluttering and sudden idyllic bursts of flight. On the last day of their honeymoon, they had gone shopping, and Walter had bought her a pair of white porcelain fantails, and they lived still at either end of her sitting-room mantelpiece. They were two of her most precious possessions.

White birds. She remembered being a child during the war, with an older brother reported missing. Fear and anxiety, like a sort of canker, had filled the house, destroying security. Until that morning when she had looked from her bedroom window and seen the gull poised on the roof of the house opposite. It was winter, and the early sun, a scarlet fireball, had just crept up into the sky, and as the gull suddenly launched itself into flight, she saw the underside of its wings stained with rosy pink. The delighted shock of such marvellous and surprising beauty filled her with comfort. She knew then that her brother was alive, and when, a week later, her parents heard officially that he was safe and well although a prisoner-of-war, they could not understand why Eve took the news so calmly. But she never told them about the gull.

And these gulls . . . ? But these were giving nothing away, no reassurances for Eve. They turned their heads, searching the empty sands, spied some distant gobbet of edible rubbish, screamed, stood tiptoe, spread their massive snowy wings and were away, wheeling and floating on the arms of the wind.

She sighed, looked at her watch. It was time to return. She whistled for the dogs, and started the long walk home.

It was nearly dark when the train drew into the station, but she saw her tall son-in-law waiting for her on the platform, standing beneath one of the lights, huddled into his old working jacket, with the collar turned up against the wind. Eve got herself out of the warm interior of the train and felt that wind, which on this particular station always seemed to blow with piercing chill, even in the middle of summer.

He came towards her. 'Eve.' They kissed. His cheek felt icy beneath her lips, and she thought he looked terrible, thinner than ever, and with no colour to his face. He stooped and picked up her suitcase. 'Is this all you've got?'

'That's all.'

Not speaking, they walked together down the platform, up the steps, out into the yard where his car waited. He opened the boot and slung her case in, then went around to unlock her door. It was not until they were away from the station and on the road that led out into the country that she steeeled herself to ask, 'How is Jane?'

'I don't know. Nobody will say for certain one way or the other. Her blood pressure soared, that's what really started it all.'

'Can I see her?'

'I asked, but not this evening, Sister said. Maybe tomorrow morning.'

There was nothing much else to be said. 'And how's Jamie?'

'He's fine. I told you, Nessie Cooper's been marvellously kind, she's been looking after him, along with her own brood.' Nessie was married to Tom Cooper, who was David's foreman. 'He's excited at the thought of you coming to look after him.'

'Dear little boy.' In the darkness of the car, she made herself smile. Her face felt as though it had not smiled for years, but it was important, for Jamie's sake, to arrive looking cheerful and calm, whatever horrors were going on in the inside of her head.

When they arrived at last, Jamie and Mrs Cooper were

watching television together in the sitting room. Jamie was in his dressing gown and drinking a mug of cocoa, but when he heard his father's voice, he set this down and came to meet them in the hall, partly because he was fond of Eve and looking forward to seeing her again, and partly because he had a very good idea that she might have brought him a present.

'Hello, Jamie.' She stooped and they kissed. He smelled of soap.

'Granny, I had lunch today with Charlie Cooper and he's six and he's got a pair of football boots.'

'Heavens above! With proper studs?'

'Yes, just like real, and he's got a football and he lets me play with him, and I can nearly do a drop kick.'

'More than I can,' Eve told him.

She pulled off her hat and began to unbutton her coat, and as she did this, Mrs Cooper emerged through the open sitting-room door and took her own coat off the hall chair.

'Nice to see you again, Mrs Douglas.'

She was a neat, slim woman, and looked far too young to be the mother of four – or was it five? – children. Eve had lost count.

'And you too, Mrs Cooper. You've been so kind. Who's looking after your lot?'

'Tom. But the baby's teething, so I must get back.'

'I can't thank you enough for all you've done.'

'Oh, it's nothing. I . . . I just hope everything goes all right.'

'I'm sure it will.'

'It doesn't seem fair, does it? I have babies, no trouble. One after the other, easy as a cat, Tom always says. and there's Mrs Murchison . . . well, I don't know. It doesn't seem fair.' She pulled on her coat and did up the buttons. 'I'll come along tomorrow to give you a hand, if you like, if you don't mind me bringing the baby. He can sit in his pram in the kitchen.'

'I'd love you to come.'

'Makes it easier, waiting,' said Mrs Cooper. 'Helps if you've got a body to talk to.'

When she had gone, Eve and Jamie went up to her bedroom and she opened her suitcase, and found his present, which was a model John Deere tractor and which he insisted politely was exactly what he had been wanting, and how had she known? With the tractor safely in his possession, he was happy to go to bed. He kissed her goodnight, and went with his father to have his teeth cleaned and be tucked into bed. Eve unpacked and washed her hands, changed her shoes and did her hair; then she went downstairs, and she and David had a drink together. She went into the kitchen and assembled a little supper for them both, which they ate off a tray by the fire. After supper, David got into the car and went back to the hospital, and Eve washed up. When this was done, she telephoned Walter, and they talked for a little, but somehow there didn't seem to be very much to say. She waited up until David returned, but still he had no news.

'They said they'd ring if anything started,' he told her. 'I want to be with her. I was with her when Jamie was born.'

'I know.' Eve smiled. 'She always said she'd never have had Jamie without you. And I told her that she'd have probably managed. Now, you look exhausted. Go to bed and try to get some sleep.'

His face was haggard with strain. 'If . . .' The words seemed to be torn from him. 'If anything happens to Jane . . .'

'It won't,' she said quickly. She laid a hand on his arm. 'You mustn't even think about it.'

'What can I think?'

'You must just have faith. And if there's a call in the middle of the night, you will come and tell me, won't you?'

26   'Of course.'

'Goodnight then, my dear.'

She had told David to sleep, but she could not sleep herself. She lay, in the downy bed, in the darkness, watching the patch of paler darkness that was the night sky beyond the drawn curtains and the open window, and listening to the hours chime by on the grandfather clock that stood at the foot of the stairs. The telephone did not ring. Dawn was breaking before at last she dozed off, and then, almost instantly, was awake again. It was half-past seven. She got up and pulled on her dressing gown and went to find Jamie, who too, was awake, sitting up in bed and playing with his tractor.

'Good morning.'

He said, 'Do you think I can play with Charlie Cooper today? I want to show him the John Deere.'

'Won't he be at school this morning?'

'This afternoon, then?'

'Perhaps.'

'What shall we do this morning?'

'What would you like to do?'

'We could go down to the foreshore and look at the geese. Do you know, Granny, do you know this, there are men who come and shoot them? Daddy hates it, but he says he can't do anything to stop them, because the foreshore belongs to everybody.'

'Wildfowlers.'

'Yes, that's right.'

'I must say it seems hard on the poor geese to fly all the way from Canada and then get shot.'

'Daddy says they *do* make an awful mess of the fields.'

'They have to feed. And talking of feeding, what do you want for breakfast?'

'Boiled eggs?'

'Up you get, then.'

In the kitchen, they found a note from David on the kitchen table:

> 7 a.m. Have fed the cattle, am just going up to the hospital again. No call during the night. I'll ring you if anything happens.

'What does he say?' asked Jamie.

'Just telling us he's gone to see your mother.'

'Has the baby come yet?'

'Not yet.'

'It's in her tummy. It's got to come out.'

'I don't expect it will be very long now.'

As they finished their breakfast, Mrs Cooper arrived with her large rosy-cheeked baby in a perambulator, which she manoeuvred into a corner of the kitchen.

She gave the baby a rusk to chew. 'Any news, Mrs Douglas?'

'No, not yet. But David's at the hospital now. He'll ring us if there's any.'

She went upstairs and made her bed, and then Jamie's, and then, after a tiny hesitation, went into Jane and David's room in order to make their bed as well.

It was impossible not to feel that she was trespassing. There was the smell of lily-of-the-valley, which was the only perfume Jane ever used. She saw the dressing table, with all Jane's small, personal possessions: her grandmother's silver hairbrushes, the snaps of David and Jamie, the strings of pretty, junky beads that she had hung from the mirror. Clothes lay about: the dungarees that she had been wearing before she was taken off in the ambulance; a pair of shoes, a scarlet sweater. She saw the childish collection of china animals, ranged along the mantelpiece, the big photograph of herself and Walter.

She turned to the bed, and saw the David had spent the night on Jane's side, with his head buried in the huge, white, lace-frilled pillow. For some reason this was the last straw. *I want her back*, she said furiously, to nobody in particular. *I want her back. I want her home, safely, with her family. I can't bear this any more. I want to know* now *that she's going to be all right.*

The telephone rang.

She sat on the edge of the bed and reached out and picked up the receiver.

'Yes?'

'Eve, it's David.'

'What's happening?'

'Nothing yet, but there seems to be a bit of a panic on and they don't want to wait any longer. She's being wheeled into the labour room now. I'm going with her. I'll call you when there's any news.'

'Yes.' *There seems to be a bit of a panic on.* 'I . . . I thought I'd take Jamie out for a walk. But we won't be long, and Mrs Cooper is here.'

'Good idea. Get him out of the house. Give him my love.'

'Take care, David.'

The foreshore lay beyond an old apple orchard, and then a field of stubble. They came to the hawthorn hedge and the stile, and then grass sloped down to the rushes and the water's edge. The tide was out, the great mudflats spread to the further shore. She saw the shallow hills and the huge sky; patches of palest blue, hung with slow-moving grey clouds.

Jamie, climbing over the stile, said, 'There are the wildfowlers.'

Eve looked and saw them, down by the edge of the water. There were two men, and they had built a hide of the brushwood that had been washed up by the high tides. They stood in this, silhouetted against the shining mudflats, their guns at the ready. A pair of brown and white springer spaniels sat nearby, waiting. It was very quiet, very still. From far out in the middle of the estuary, Eve could hear the chatter and gobble of the wild geese.

She helped Jamie off the stile, and hand in hand they made their way down the slope. Where this levelled off they came to a group of plaster birds which the wildfowlers had arranged to resemble a flock of feeding geese.

'They're toy ones,' said Jamie.

'They're decoys. The wildfowlers hope that any geese that fly over will see them and think it's safe to come down and feed.'

'I think that's horrid. I think that's cheating. If any come, Granny, if any come, let's wave our arms and chase them away.'

'I don't think we'll be very popular if we do.'

'Let's tell the wildfowlers to go away.'

'We can't do that. They're not breaking any law.'

'They're shooting our geese.'

'The wild geese belong to everybody.'

The wildfowlers had seen them. The dogs had their ears pricked and were wheeking. One of the men swore at his dog. Nonplussed, not knowing now quite which way to go, Eve and Jamie stood by the ring of decoys, hesitating, and as they did this, a movement in the sky caught Eve's eye and she looked up, and saw, coming from the direction of the sea, a line of birds.

'Look, Jamie.'

The wildfowlers had seen them, too. There was a stir of activity as they turned to face the incoming flight.

'Don't let them come!' Jamie sounded panic-stricken. He pulled his hand free from Eve's, and began to run, stumbling on his short, gum-booted legs, waving his arms, trying to divert the distant birds and turn them away from the guns. 'Go away, go away, don't come!'

Eve felt that she should try to stop him, but there seemed little point. Nothing on earth could halt that relentless flight. And, as well, there was something unusual about these birds. The wild geese flew from north to south on regular flight lines, but this flock approached from the east, from the sea, and with every second they grew larger. For an instant Eve's natural measure of distance was both dazzled and baffled, and then it all clicked into true focus, and she saw that the birds were not geese at all, but twelve white swans.

'They're swans, Jamie. They're swans.'

He heard her and stopped dead, standing silently, his head bent back to watch them fly over. They came, and the air was filled with the drumming and beating of their immense wings. She saw the long white necks stretched forward, the legs tucked up and streaming behind. And then they were over and gone, flying upriver, and the sound of their wings died into the silence, and finally they disappeared, swallowed into the greyness of the morning, the distance of the hills.

'Granny.' Jamie caught her sleeve and shook it. 'Granny, you're not listening.' She looked down at him. It felt like looking down at a child she had never seen before. 'Granny, the wildfowlers didn't shoot them.'

Twelve white swans. 'They're not allowed to shoot swans. Swans belong to the Queen.'

'I'm glad. I thought they were *beauti*-ful.'

'Yes. Yes, they were.'

'Where do you think they're going?'

'I don't know. Up the river. Up to the hills. Perhaps there's a hidden loch where they feed and nest.' But she spoke absently, because she was not thinking about the swans. She was thinking about Jane, and all at once it was intensely urgent that they lose no time at all in getting home.

'Come along, Jamie.' She took his hand, and began to scramble back up the grassy slope towards the stile, dragging him behind her. 'Let's go back.'

'But we haven't had our walk yet.'

'We've walked far enough. Let's hurry. Hurry. Let's see how quick we can be.'

They climbed the stile and ran across the stubble, Jamie's short legs doing their valiant best to keep up with his grandmother's. They went through the orchard, not stopping to look for windfalls or to climb the wizened old trees. Not stopping for anything.

Now, they reached the track that led to the farmhouse and Jamie was exhausted, he could run no further and stopped dead in protest at such extraordinary behaviour. But Eve could not bear to linger, and she swung him up into her arms and hurried on, not minding his weight, scarcely noticing it.

They came to the house at last, and went in through the back door, not even stopping to take off their muddy boots. Through the back porch, into the warm kitchen, where the baby still sat placidly in its perambulator and Mrs Cooper peeled potatoes at the kitchen sink. She turned as they approached, and as she did this, the telephone began to ring. Eve set Jamie down on his feet and darted to answer it. It had only time to ring once more before she had picked up the receiver.

'Yes.'

'Eve, it's David. It's all over. Everything's all right. We've got another little boy. He had a pretty rough ride, but he's strong and healthy and Jane's fine. A bit tired, but they've got her back into bed, and you can come and see her this afternoon.'

'Oh, *David* . . .'

'Can I speak to Jamie?'

'Of course.'

She handed the little boy the receiver. 'It's Daddy. You've got a brother.' She turned to Mrs Cooper, who was still standing with a knife in one hand and a potato in the other. 'She's all right, Mrs Cooper. She's all right.' She wanted to hug Mrs Cooper, to press kisses on her rosy cheeks. 'It's a little boy, and nothing went wrong. She's all right . . . and . . .'

It wasn't any good. She couldn't say any more. And she could no longer see Mrs Cooper because her eyes had filled with tears. She never cried, and she did not want Jamie to see her crying, so she turned and left Mrs Cooper standing there, and simply went out of the kitchen, out the way they had come in, out into the garden and the cold, fresh morning air.

It was safely over. Relief made her feel so weightless it was as though she could have taken a single leap and floated up, ten or twenty feet into the air. She was crying, but she was laughing too, which was ridiculous, so she felt in her pocket and found a handkerchief, and wiped her eyes and blew her nose.

Twelve white swans. She was glad that Jamie had been with her, otherwise, for the rest of her life, she might have suspected that that astonishing sight had been simply a figment of her own overwrought imagintion. Twelve white swans. She had watched them come and watched them go. Gone forever. She knew that she would not witness such a miraculous sight again.

She looked up into the empty sky. It had clouded over, and soon it would probably start to rain. As the thought occurred to her, Eve felt the first cold wet drops upon her face. Twelve white swans. She buried her hands deep in the pockets of her coat, and turned and went indoors to telephone her husband.

THE TREE

The Tree

At five o'clock on a sultry, sizzling London afternoon in July, Jill Armitage, pushing the baby buggy that contained her small son Robbie, emerged through the gates of the park and started to walk the mile of pavements that led to home.

It was a small park and not a very spectacular one. The grass was trodden, the paths fouled by other people's dogs, the flower beds filled with things like lobelia and hot red geraniums and strange plants with beetroot-coloured leaves, but at least there was a children's corner, and a shady tree or two, and some swings and a see-saw.

She had packed a basket with some toys and a token picnic for the two of them, and this was now slung on the handles of the buggy. All that could be seen of her child was the top of his cotton sun hat and his red canvas sneakers. He wore a skimpy pair of shorts and his arms and shoulders were the colour of apricots. She hoped that he had not caught the sun. His thumb was in his mouth, he hummed to himself, *meh, meh, meh*, a sound he made when he was sleepy.

They came to the main road and stood, waiting to cross. Traffic, two lanes deep, poured in front of them. Sunlight flashed on windscreens, drivers were in shirt sleeves, the air was heavy with the smell of exhaust and petrol fumes.

The lights changed, brakes screeched, and traffic halted. Jill pushed the buggy across the road. On the far side was the greengrocer's shop, and Jill thought about supper that evening, and went in to buy a lettuce and a pound of tomatoes. The man who served her was an old friend – living in this run-down corner of London was a little like living in a village – and he called Robbie 'My love' and gave him, free, a peach for his supper.

Jill thanked the greengrocer and trudged on. Before long she turned into her own street, where the Georgian houses had once been quite grand, and the pavements were wide and flagged with stone. Since getting married and coming to live in the neighbourhood, she had learned to take for granted the decrepitude of everything, the dingy paint, the broken railings, the sinister basements with their grubby drawn curtains and damp stone steps sprouting ferns. But over the last two years, hopeful signs of improvement had begun to show in the street. Here, a house changed hands intact, scaffolding went up, great Council skips stood at the road's edge and were filled with all sorts of interesting rubbish. There, a basement flat sported a new coat of white paint, and a honeysuckle was planted in a tub, and in no time at all had reached the railings, twisting and twining with branches laden with blossom. Gradually, windows were being replaced, lintels repaired, front doors painted shiny black or cornflower blue, brass handles and letter boxes polished to a shine. A new and expensive breed of car stood at the pavement's edge and a whole new and expensive breed of mothers walked their offspring to the corner shop, or brought them home from parties, carrying balloons and wearing false noses and paper hats.

Ian said that the district was going up in the world, but really, it was just that people could no longer afford to buy property in Fulham or Kensington, and had started to try their luck further afield.

Ian and Jill had bought their house when they were married, three years ago, but still they had the dead weight of a mortgage hanging around their necks, and since Robbie was born and Jill had stopped working, their financial problems were even more acute. And now, to make matters worse, there was another baby on the way. They had wanted another baby; they had planned for another baby, but perhaps not quite so soon.

'Never mind,' Ian had said when he got over the shock. 'We'll have it all over and done with in one fell swoop, and just think what fun the children will be for each other, only two years apart.'

'I just feel we can't afford it.'

'It doesn't cost anything to have a baby.'

'No, but it costs a lot to bring them up. And buy them shoes. Do you know what it costs to buy Robbie a pair of sandals?'

Ian said that he didn't know and he didn't want to. They would manage somehow. He was an eternal optimist and the best thing about his optimism was that it was catching. He gave his wife a kiss and went out to the off-licence around the corner and bought a bottle of wine which they drank that evening, with their supper of sausage and mash.

'At least we've got a roof over our heads,' he told her, 'even if most of it belongs to the Building Society.'

And so they had, but even their best friends had to admit that it was an odd house. For the street, at its end, turned in a sharp curve, and Number 23, where Jill and Ian lived, was tall and thin, wedge-shaped in order to accommodate the angle of the bend. It was its very oddness that had attracted them in the first place, as well as its price; for it had been allowed to reach a sad state of dilapidation and needed much done to it. Its very oddness was part of its charm, but charm didn't help much when they had run out of the time, energy, and means to attend to the outside painting, or apply a coat of Snowcem to its narrow frontage.

Only the basement, paradoxically, sparkled. This was where Delphine, their lodger, lived. Delphine's rent helped to pay the mortgage. She was a painter who had turned, with some success, to commercial art, and she used the basement as a London pied-à-terre, commuting between this and a cottage in Wiltshire, where a decrepit barn had been converted into a studio, and an overgrown garden sloped down on the reedy banks of a small river. Every so often, Jill and Ian and Robbie were invited to this enchanting place for a weekend, and these visits were always the greatest treat – a feast of ill-assorted guests, enormous meals, quantities of wine, and endless discussions on esoteric subjects usually quite beyond Jill's comprehension. They made, as Ian was wont to point out when they returned to humdrum old London, a nice change.

Delphine, enormously fat in her flowing caftan, was sitting now outside her own front door, basking in the shaft of sunlight which, at this time of the day, penetrated her domain. Jill lifted Robbie out of the buggy, and Robbie stuck his head through the railings and stared down at Delphine, who put down her newspaper and stared back at him from behind round, black sunglasses.

'Hello, there,' she said. 'Where have you been?'

'To the park,' Jill told her.

'In this heat?'

'There's nowhere else to go.'

'You should do something about the garden.'

Delphine had been saying this, at intervals, over the last two years, until Ian told her that if she said it once more, he, personally, would strangle her. 'Cut down that horrible tree.'

'Don't start on that,' Jill pleaded. 'It's all too difficult.'

'Well, at least you could get rid of the cats. I could hardly sleep last night for the yowling.'

40 'What can we do?'

'Anything. Get a gun and shoot them.'

'Ian hasn't got a gun. And even if he had, the police would think we were murdering someone if we started blasting off at cats.'

'What a loyal little wife you are. Well, if you won't shoot the cats, how about coming down to the cottage this weekend? I'll drive the lot of you in my car.'

'Oh, Delphine.' It was the best thing that had happened all day. 'Do you really mean it?'

'Of course.' Jill thought of the cool country garden, the smell of elderflowers; of letting Robbie paddle his feet in the shallow pebbly waters of the river.

'I can't think of anything more heavenly . . . but I'll have to see what Ian says. He might be playing cricket.'

'Come down after dinner and I'll give you both a glass of wine. We'll discuss it then.'

By six o'clock, Robbie was bathed, fed – on the juicy peach – and asleep in his cot. Jill took a shower, put on the coolest garment she owned, which was a cotton dressing gown, and went down to the kitchen to do something about supper.

The kitchen and the dining room, divided only by the narrow staircase, took up the entire ground floor of the house, but still were not large. The front door led straight into this, so that there never seemed to be anywhere to hang coats or park a pram. At the dining-room end, the window faced out onto the street; but the kitchen had enormous French windows of glass, which seemed to indicate that once there had been a balcony beyond, with perhaps a flight of steps leading down into the garden. The balcony and the steps had long since disintegrated – been demolished, perhaps – disappeared, and the French windows opened onto nothing but a twenty-foot drop to the yard beneath. Before Robbie was born they used to let the window stand open in warm weather, but after his arrival, Ian, for safety, nailed them shut, and so they had stayed.

The scrubbed pine table stood against these windows. Jill sat at it and sliced tomatoes for the salad in a preoccupied sort of way, gazing down at the horrible garden. Encased as it was by high, crumbling brick walls, it was a little like looking down into the bottom of a well. Near the house there was the brick yard, and then a patch of straggling grass, and then desolation, trodden earth, old paper bags that kept blowing in, and the tree.

Jill had been born and brought up in the country and found it hard to believe that she could actually dislike a garden. So much so that even if there had been any form of access, she would not hang her washing out, let alone allow her child to play there.

And as for the tree – she positively hated the tree. It was a sycamore, but light-years away from the friendly sycamores she remembered from her childhood, good for climbing, shady in summer, scattering winged seed-pods in the autumn. This one should never have grown at all; should never have been planted, should never have reached such a height, such density, such sombre, depressing size. It shut out the sky, and its gloom discouraged all life except the cats, who prowled, howling, along the tops of the walls and used the sparse earth as their lavatories. In the autumn, when the leaves fell from the tree and Ian braved the cats' messes to go out and build a bonfire, the resultant smoke was black and stinking, as though the leaves had absorbed, during the summer months, everything in the air that was dirty, repellent, or poisonous.

Their marriage was a happy one, and most of the time Jill wanted nothing to be different. But the tree brought out the worst in her, made her long to be rich, so that she could damn the expense and get rid of it.

Sometimes she said this, aloud, to Ian. 'I wish I had an enormous private income of my own. Or that I had a marvellously wealthy relation. Then I could get the tree cut down. Why hasn't one of us got a fairy godmother? Haven't you got one hidden away?'

'You know I only have Edwin Makepeace, and he's about as much good as a wet weekend in November.'

Edwin Makepeace was a family joke, and how Ian's parents had ever been impelled to make him godfather to their son was an enigma that Jill had never got around to solving. He was some sort of a distant cousin, and had always had a reputation for being humourless, demanding, and paranoically mean with his money. The passing years had done nothing to remedy any of these traits. He had been married, for a number of years, to a dull lady called Gladys. They had had no children, simply lived together in a small house in Woking renowned for its gloom, but at least Gladys had looked after him, and when she died and he was left alone, the problem of Edwin became a constant niggle on the edge of the family's conscience.

Poor old chap, they would say, and hope that somebody else would ask him for Christmas. The somebody else who did so was usually Ian's mother, who was a truly kind-hearted lady, and it took some determination on her part not to allow Edwin's depressing presence to totally dampen the family festivities. The fact that he gave her no more than a box of hankies, which she never used, did nothing to endear him to the rest of the party. It wasn't, as they pointed out, that Edwin didn't have any money. It was just that he didn't like parting with it.

'Perhaps we could cut down the tree ourselves.'

'Darling, it's much too big. We'd either kill ourselves or knock the whole house down.'

'We could get a professional. A tree surgeon.'

'And what would we do with the bones when the surgeon had done his job?'

'A bonfire?'

'A bonfire. That size? The whole terrace would go up in smoke.'

'We could *ask* somebody. We could get an estimate.'

'My love, I can give you an estimate. It would cost a bomb. And we haven't got a bomb.'

'A garden. It would be like having another room. Space for Robbie to play. And I could put the new baby out in a pram.'

'How? Lower it from the kitchen window on a rope?'

They had had this conversation, with varying degrees of acrimony, too many times.

I'm not going to mention it again, Jill promised herself, but . . . She stopped slicing the tomato, sat with the knife in one hand and her chin resting on the other hand, and gazed out through the grimy window, that couldn't be cleaned because there was no way of getting at it.

The tree. Her imagination removed it; but then what did one do with what remained? What would ever grow in that bitter scrap of earth? How could they keep the cats away? She was still mulling over these insuperable problems when there came the sound of her husband's latchkey in the lock. She jumped, as though she had been caught doing something indecent, and quickly started slicing the tomato again. The door banged shut and she looked up over her shoulder to smile at him.

'Hello, darling.'

He dumped his briefcase, came to kiss her. He said, 'God, what a furnace of a day. I'm filthy, and I smell. I'm going to have a shower, and then I shall come and be charming to you . . .'

44 'There's a can of lager in the fridge.'

'Riches indeed,' he kissed her again. 'You, on the other hand, smell delicious. Of freesias.' He began to pull his tie loose.

'It's the soap.'

He made for the stairs, undressing himself as he went. 'Let's hope it does the same for me.'

Five minutes later he was down again, bare-footed, wearing an old pair of faded jeans and a short-sleeved shirt he had bought for his honeymoon.

'Robbie's asleep,' he told her. 'I just looked in.' He opened the fridge, took out the can of lager and poured it into two glasses, then brought them over to the table and collapsed into a chair beside her. 'What did you do today?'

She told him about going to the park, about the free peach, about Delphine's invitation for the weekend. 'She said she'd drive us down in her car.'

'She is an angel. What a marvellous thought.'

'She's asked us down for a glass of wine after dinner. She said we could talk about it.'

'A little party, in fact.'

'Oh, well, it makes a nice change.'

They looked at each other, smiling. He put out a hand and laid it on her flat and slender stomach. He said, 'For a pregnant lady, you look very toothsome.' He ate a piece of tomato. 'Is this dinner, or are we defrosting the fridge?'

'It's dinner. With some cold ham and potato salad.'

'I'm starving. Let's eat it and then go and beat Delphine up. You did say she was going to open a bottle of wine?'

'That's what she said.'

He yawned. 'Better if it was two.'

The next day was Thursday and as hot as ever, but somehow now it didn't matter, because there was the weekend to look forward to.

'We're going to Wiltshire,' Jill told Robbie, flinging a load of clothes into the washing machine. 'You'll be able to paddle in the river and pick flowers. Do you remember Wiltshire? Do you remember Delphine's cottage? Do you remember the tractor in the field?'

Robbie said 'Tractor.' He didn't have many words, but this was one of them. He smiled as he said it.

'That's right. We're going to the country.' She began to pack, because although the trip was a day away, it made the weekend seem nearer. She ironed her best sundress, she even ironed Ian's oldest T-shirt. 'We're going to stay with Delphine.' She was extravagant and bought a cold chicken for supper and a little punnet of strawberries. There would be strawberries growing in Delphine's wild garden. She thought of going out to pick them, the sun hot on her back, the rosy fruits fragrant beneath their sheltering leaves.

The day drew to a close. She bathed Robbie and read to him and put him in his cot. As she left him, his eyes already drooping, she heard Ian's key in the latch and ran downstairs to welcome him.

'Darling.'

He put down his briefcase and shut the door. His expression was bleak. She kissed him quickly and said, 'What's wrong?'

'I'm afraid something rotten has come up. Would you mind most dreadfully if we didn't go to Delphine's?'

'Not go?' Disappointment made her feel weak and emptied as though all her happiness were being drained out of her. She could not keep the dismay out of her face. 'But – oh, Ian, why not?'

'My mother rang me at the office.' He pulled off his jacket and slung it over the end of the banister. He began to loosen his tie. 'It's Edwin.'

'Edwin?' Jill's legs shook. She sat on the stairs. 'He's not *dead*?'

'No, he's not, but apparently, he's not been too well lately. He's been told by the doctor to take things easy. But now his best friend has what Edwin calls "passed on", and the funeral's on Saturday and Edwin insists on coming to London to be there. My mother tried to talk him out of it, but he won't budge. He's booked himself in for the night at some grotty, cheap hotel and Ma's convinced he's going to have a heart attack and die too. But the nub of the matter is that he's got it into his head that he'd like to come and have dinner with us. I told her that it was just because he'd rather have a free meal than one he has to pay for, but she swears it's not that at all. He kept saying he never sees anything of you and me, he's never seen our house, he wants to get to know Robbie . . . you know the sort of thing . . .'

When Ian was upset, he always talked too much. After a little Jill said, 'Do we *have* to? I wanted so much to go to the country.'

'I know. But if I explain to Delphine, I know she'll understand, give us a rain check.'

'It's just that . . .' She was near to tears. 'It's just that nothing nice or exciting ever happens to us nowadays. And when it does, we can't do it because of somebody like Edwin. Why should it be us? Why can't somebody else look after him?'

'I suppose it's because he doesn't have that number of friends?'

Jill looked up at him, and saw her own disappointment and indecision mirrored in his face.

She said, knowing what the outcome would inevitably be, 'Do you want him to come?'

Ian shrugged, miserably. 'He's my godfather.'

'It would be bad enough if he was a jolly old man, but he's so gloomy.'

'He's old. And lonely.'

'He's dull.'

'He's sad. His best friend's just died.'

'Did you tell your mother we were meant to be going to Wiltshire?'

'Yes. And she said that we had to talk it over. I said I'd ring Edwin this evening.'

'We can't tell him *not* to come.'

'That's what I thought you'd say.' They gazed at each other, knowing that the decision was made; behind them. No country weekend. No strawberries to be picked. No garden for Robbie. Just Edwin.

She said, 'I wish it wasn't so hard to do good deeds. I wish they just happened, without one having to do anything about them.'

'They wouldn't be good deeds if they happened that way. But you know something? I do love you. More, all the time, if possible.' He stooped and kissed her. 'Well . . .' He turned and opened the door again. 'I'd better go down and tell Delphine.'

'There's cold chicken for supper.'

'In that case I'll see if I can rustle up enough loose change for a bottle of wine. We both need cheering up.'

Once the dreadful disappointment had been conquered Jill decided to follow her own mother's philosophy – if a thing is worth doing, it's worth doing well. So what, if it was only dreary old Edwin Makepeace, fresh from a funeral; it was still a dinner party. She made a cassoulet of chicken and herbs, scrubbed new potatoes, concocted a sauce for the broccoli. For dessert there was fresh fruit salad, and then a creamy wedge of Brie.

She polished the gate-leg table in the dining room, laid it with the best mats, arranged flowers (bought late yesterday from the stall in the market), plumped up the patchwork cushions in the first-floor sitting room.

Ian had gone to fetch Edwin. He had said, his voice sounding shaky over the telephone, that he would take a taxi, but Ian knew that it would cost him ten pounds or more and had insisted on making the journey himself. Jill bathed Robbie and dressed him in his new pyjamas, and then changed herself into the freshly ironed sundress that had been intended for Wiltshire. (She put out of her mind the image of Delphine, setting off in her car with no one for company but her easel and her weekend bags. The sun would go on shining; the heatwave would continue. They would be invited again, for another weekend.)

Now, all was ready. Jill and Robbie knelt on the sofa that stood in the living-room bay window, and watched for Edwin's arrival. When the car drew up, she gathered Robbie into her arms and went downstairs to open the door. Edwin was coming up the steps from the street, with Ian behind him. Jill had not seen him since last Christmas and thought that he had aged considerably. She did not remember that he had had to walk with a cane. He wore a black tie and a relentless dark suit. He carried no small gift, no flowers, no bottle of wine. He looked like an undertaker.

'Edwin.'

'Well, my dear, here we are. This is very good of you.'

He came into the house, and she gave him a kiss. His old skin felt rough and dry and he smelt, vaguely, of disinfectant, like an old-fashioned doctor. He was a very thin man; his eyes, which had once been a cold blue, were now faded and rheumy. There was high colour on his cheekbones, but otherwise he looked bloodless, monochrome. His stiff collar seemed a good size too large, and his neck was stringy as a turkey's.

'I was so sorry to hear about your friend.' She felt that it was 49 important to get this said at once.

'Oh, well, it comes to all of us, yerknow. Three score years and ten, that's our alloted span, and Edgar was seventy-three. I'm seventy-one. Now, where shall I put my stick?'

There wasn't anywhere, so she took it from him and hung it on the end of the banister.

He looked about him. He had probably never before seen an open-plan house.

'Well, look at this. And this' – he leaned forward, his beak of a nose pointing straight into Robbie's face – 'is your son.'

Jill wondered if Robbie would let her down and burst into tears of fright. He did not, however, simply stared back into Edwin's face with unblinking eyes.

'I . . . I kept him up. I thought you'd like to meet each other. But he's rather sleepy.' Ian now came through the door and shut it behind him. 'Would you like to come upstairs?'

She led the way, and he followed her, a step at a time, and she heard his laboured breathing. In the sitting room she set the little boy down, and pulled up a chair for Edwin. 'Why don't you sit here?'

He sat, cautiously. Ian offered him a glass of sherry, and Jill left them, and took Robbie upstairs to put him into his cot.

He said, just before he put his thumb into his mouth, 'Nose,' and she was filled with love for him making her want to laugh.

'I know,' she whispered. 'He *has* got a big nose, hasn't he?'

He smiled back, his eyes drooped. She put up the side of the cot and went downstairs. Edwin was still on about his old friend. 'We were in the Army together during the war. Army Pay Corps. After the war, he went back to Insurance, but we always kept in touch. Went on holiday once together, Gladys and Edgar and myself. He never married. Went to Budleigh Salterton.' He eyed Ian over his sherry glass. 'Ever been to Budleigh Salterton?'

Ian said that no, he had never been to Budleigh Salterton.

'Pretty place. Good golf course. Of course, Edgar was never much of a man for golf. Tennis when we were younger, and then he took up bowls. Ever played bowls, Ian?'

Ian said that no, he had never played bowls.

'No,' said Edwin. 'You wouldn't have. Cricket's yer game, isn't it?'

'When I can get the chance.'

'Yer probably pretty busy.'

'Yes, pretty busy.'

'Play at weekends, I expect.'

'Sometimes.'

'I watched the Test Match on my television set.' He took another cautious sip at his Tio Pepe, his lips puckered. 'Didn't think much of the Pakistanis.'

Jill, discreetly, got to her feet and went downstairs to the kitchen. When she called to them that dinner was ready, Edwin was still talking about cricket, recalling some match in 1956 that he had particularly enjoyed. The drone of this long story was stilled by her interruption. Presently the two men came down the stairs. Jill was at the table, lighting the candles.

'Never been in a house like this,' observed Edwin, sitting down and unfolding his napkin. 'How much did yer pay for it?'

Ian, after a tiny hesitation, told him.

'When did yer buy it?'

'When we were married. Three years ago.'

'Yer didn't do too badly.'

'It was in rotten shape. It's still not great shakes, but we'll get it straight in time.'

Jill found Edwin's disconcerting stare directed at herself. 'Yer mother-in-law tells me yer having another baby.'

'Oh. Well . . . yes, I am.'

'Not meant to be a secret, is it?'

'No. No, of course not.' She picked up the cassoulet in oven-gloved hands and pushed it at him. 'It's chicken.'

'Always fond of chicken. We used to have chicken in India during the war . . .' He was off again. 'Funny thing, how good the Indians were at cooking chicken. Suppose they had a lot of practice. Yer weren't allowed to eat the cows. Sacred, you see . . .'

Ian opened the wine, and after that things got a little easier. Edwin refused the fruit salad, but ate most of the Brie. And all the time he talked, seeming to need no sort of response, merely a nod of the head or an attentive smile. He talked about India, about a friend he had made in Bombay; about a tennis match he had once played in Camberley; about Gladys's aunt, who had taken up loom-weaving and had won a prize at the Country Show.

The long, hot evening wore on. The sun slid out of the hazed city sky, and left it stained with pink. Edwin was now complaining of his daily help's inability to fry eggs properly, and all at once Ian excused himself, got to his feet, and took himself off to the kitchen to make coffee.

Edwin, interrupted in his free flow, watched him go. 'That yer kitchen?' he asked.

'Yes.'

'Let's have a look at it.' And before she could stop him, he had hauled himself to his feet and was headed after Ian. She followed him, but he would not be diverted upstairs.

'Not much room, have you?'

'It's all right,' said Ian. Edwin went to the French windows and peered out through the grimy glass.

'What's this?'

'It's . . .' Jill joined him, gazing in an agonised fashion at the familiar horror below. 'It's the garden. Only we don't use it because it's rather nasty. The cats come and make messes. And anyway, we can't get to it. As you can see,' she finished tamely.

'What about the basement?'

'The basement's let. To a friend. Called Delphine.'

'Doesn't she mind living cheek-by-jowl with a tip like that?'

'She's — she's not here very often. She's usually in the country.'

'Hmm.' There was a long, disconcerting silence. Edwin looked at the tree, his eyes travelling from its grubby roots to the topmost branches. His nose was like a pointer and all the sinews in his neck stood out like ropes.

'Why don't yer cut the tree down?'

Jill sent an agonised glance in Ian's direction. Behind Edwin's back, he threw his eyes to heaven, but he said, reasonably enough, 'It would be rather difficult. As you can see, it's very large.'

'Horrible, having a tree like that in yer garden.'

'Yes,' agreed Jill. 'It's not very convenient.'

'Why don't yer do something about it?'

Ian said quickly, 'Coffee's ready. Let's go upstairs.'

Edwin turned on him. 'I said, why don't yer do something about it?'

'I will,' said Ian. 'One day.'

'No good waiting for one day. One day yer'll be as old as me and the tree will still be there.'

'Coffee?' said Ian.

'And the cats are unhealthy. Unhealthy when children are about the place.'

'I don't let Robbie out in the garden,' Jill told him. 'I couldn't even if I wanted to, because there is no way we can get to it. I think there used to be a balcony and steps down to the garden, but they'd gone before we bought the house, and somehow . . . well, we've never got around to doing anything about replacing them.' She was determined that she would not make

53

it sound as though she and Ian were penniless and pathetic. 'I mean, there's been so much else to do.'

Edwin said 'Hmm' again. He stood, his hands in his pockets, gazing through the window, and after a bit Jill wondered if he was drifting off into some sort of a coma. But then he became brisk, took his hands out of his pockets, turned to Ian and said, testily, 'I thought you were making us coffee, Ian. How long do we have to wait for it?'

He stayed for another hour, and his endless flow of deadly anecdote never ceased. At last the clock from a neighbouring church began to chime eleven o'clock, and Edwin set down his coffee cup, glanced at his own watch, and announced that it was time for Ian to drive him back to his hotel. They all went downstairs. Ian found his car keys and opened the door. Jill gave Edwin his stick.

'Been a pleasant evening. Liked seeing yer house.'

She kissed him again. He went out and down the steps and crossed the pavement. Ian, trying not to look too eager, stood with the door of the car open. The old man cautiously got in, stowed his legs and his stick. Ian shut the door and went around to the driving seat. Jill, smiling still, waved them off. When the car disappeared around the corner at the end of the street, and not before, she let the smile drop, and went inside, exhausted, to start in on the washing up.

In bed that night, 'He wasn't too bad,' said Jill.

'I suppose not. But he takes everything so for granted, as though we all owed him something. He could at least have brought you a single red rose, or a bar of chocolate.'

'He's just not that sort of a person.'

'And his stories! Poor old Edwin, I think he was born a bore. He's so terribly good at it. He probably Bored for his school, and went on to Bore for England. Probably captained the team.'

'At least we didn't have to think of things to say.'

'It was a delicious dinner, and you were sweet to him.' He yawned enormously and heaved himself over, longing for sleep. 'Anyway, we did it. That's the last of it.'

But in that Ian was wrong. That was not the last of it, although two weeks passed by before anything happened. A Friday again, and as usual Jill was in the kitchen, getting supper ready, when Ian returned home from the office.

'Hello, darling.'

He shut the door, dumped his briefcase, came to kiss her. He pulled out a chair and sat down, and they faced each other across the table. He said, 'The most extraordinary thing has happened.'

Jill was instantly apprehensive. 'Nice extraordinary or horrid extraordinary?'

He grinned, put his hand in his pocket, and pulled out a letter. He tossed it across to her. 'Read that.'

Mystified, Jill picked it up and unfolded it. It was a long letter and typewritten. It was from Edwin.

My dear Ian

This is to thank you for the pleasant evening with you both, and the excellent dinner, and to say how much I appreciated your motoring me to and fro. I must say that it goes against the grain, being forced to pay exorbitant taxi fares. I much enjoyed meeting your child and seeing your house. You have, however, an obvious problem with your garden, and I have given the matter some thought.

Your first priority is obviously to get rid of the tree. On no account must you tackle it yourself. There are a number of professional firms in London who are qualified to deal with such work, and I have taken the liberty of instructing three of them to call on you, at your convenience, and give you estimates. Once the tree has gone, you will have more idea of the possibilities of your plot, but in the meantime I would suggest the following:

The letter continued, by now reading like a builder's specification. Existing walls made good, repointed, and painted white. A trellis fence, for privacy, erected along the top of these walls. The ground cleared and levelled, and laid with flags – a drain to be discreetly incorporated in one corner for easy cleaning. Outside the kitchen window a wooden deck – preferably teak – to be erected, supported by steel joists, and with an open wooden staircase giving access to the garden below.

I think [Edwin continued] this more or less covers the structural necessities. You may want to construct a raised flower bed along one of the walls, or make a small rockery around the stump of the removed tree, but this is obviously up to yourselves.

Which leaves us with the problem of the cats. Again, I have made some enquiries and discovered that there is an excellent repellant which is safe to use where there are children about. A squirt or two of this should do the trick, and once the soil and grass have been covered by flags, I see no reason why cats should return for any function, natural or otherwise.

This is obviously going to cost quite a lot of money. I realise that, with inflation and the rising cost of living, it is not always easy for a young couple, however hard they work, to make ends meet. And I should like to help. I have, in fact, made provision for you in my Will, but it occurs to me that it would be much more in keeping to hand the money over to you now. Then you will be able to deal with your garden, and I shall have the pleasure of seeing it completed, hopefully before I, too, follow my good friend Edgar, and pass on.

Finally, your mother indicated to me that you had given up a pleasurable weekend in order to cheer me up on the evening of Edgar's funeral. Your kindness equals her own, and I am fortunate to be in a financial position when I am able, at last, to repay my debts.

With best wishes,

Yours

Edwin

Edwin. She could hardly see his spiky signature because her eyes were full of tears. She imagined him, sitting in his dark little house in Woking, absorbed in their problems, working them all out; taking time to look up suitable firms, probably making endless telephone calls, doing little sums, forgetting no tiny detail, taking trouble . . .

'Well?' said Ian, gently.

The tears had started to slide down her cheeks. She put up a hand and tried to wipe them away.

'I never thought. I never thought he'd do anything like *this*. Oh, Ian, and we've been so horrible about him.'

'You were never horrible. You wouldn't know how to be horrible about anybody.'

'I . . . I never imagined he had any money at all.'

'I don't think any of us did. Not that sort of money.'

'How can we ever thank him?'

'By doing what he says. By doing just exactly what he's told us to do, and then asking him around to the garden-warming. We'll throw a little party.' He grinned. 'It'll make a nice change.'

She looked out of the window, through the grimy glass. A paper bag had found its way into the garden from some neighbouring dustbin, and the nastiest of the tom cats, the one with the torn ear, was sitting on top of the wall, eyeing her.

She met his cold green stare with equanimity. She said, 'I'll be able to hang out my washing. I shall get some tubs, and plant bulbs for the spring, and pink ivy-leafed geranium in the summer. And Robbie can play there and we'll have a sandpit. And if the deck is big enough, I can even put the baby out there, in the pram. Oh, Ian, isn't it going to be *wonderful*? I won't ever have to go to the park again. Just think.'

'You know what I think?' said Ian. 'I think it would be a good idea to go and give old Edwin a ring.'

So they went together to the telephone and dialled Edwin's number, and stood very close, with their arms around each other, waiting for the old gentleman to answer their call.

A Note on Rosamunde Pilcher

Rosamunde Pilcher was encouraged to write from an early age and had her first story published in *Woman and Home* at the age of eighteen. During the Second World War, she worked first in the Foreign Office and then in the Women's Royal Naval Service, serving in Portsmouth and Trincomalee, Ceylon, with the East India fleet. After the war she married and moved to Scotland. She and her husband today live near Dundee. They have four children and eight grandchildren. Throughout this time Rosamunde Pilcher has been writing continuously, for magazines as well as thirteen novels and two volumes of short stories.

Rosamunde Pilcher's *The Shell Seekers* marked her entrance to the realm of bestselling novelists. Her two other novels are *September* and *Coming Home*.